A Visitor in the Dark

as told by Eddie Spaghetti

written by Ed Bisiar

illustrated by Tisha L. Adams

ISBN 0-9753091-0-2

First Published by Bisiar Music Publishing, 2004

Bisiar Music Publishing
P.O. Box 424
Evergreen, CO 80437

THE AUTHOR

Eddie Spaghetti (aka., Ed Bisiar) is this righteous dude who sings and dances for anyone who will sit still to see him. He has written and performed a multitude of whimsical, funny, and maybe even profound songs and stories for several decades and has just now (to the delight of his fans) decided to put one of his stories, told in his shows, into book form. Ta-Da! This is it. Eddie hopes you enjoy reading this tale, and telling it to those who may be a bit skittish about going to sleep, all alone ... in the dark ...

WEB SITE: EddieSpaghettiUSA.com

THE ILLUSTRATOR

Tisha L. Adams is an Art Therapist, teacher, and artist. Her passion is helping children experience the wonderment, nourishment, and enjoyment of art. She believes that art, play, and humor are the basic ingredients of a healthful life
WEB SITE: You may contact Tisha through www.EddieSpaghettiUSA.com

Consulting on and preparation of this publishing effort was completed by Joan Garne Art Design of Littleton, Colorado.
WEB SITE: www.JoanGarnerArtDesign.com

Visit (in the dark if you like)
Eddie Spaghetti at:

www.EddieSpaghettiUSA.com

Additional songs and materials, scheduling and booking of performances can be obtained there.

This book is dedicated to my two children, Christa and Terry, who are now adults and who continue to be an inspiration.

She kissed him goodnight
And tucked in his cover.
And did what you do
for a son as a mother.

"Sweet dreams. I love you. Sleep tight and good night."

Then she made
the room dark

as she turned

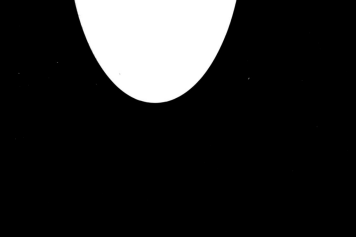

out the light.

As he lay there in the darkness,
peering over his sheet,
He saw something move –
in the corner – by his feet!

8

It was **CREEPING**,
It was *crawling*;
It was moving his way.

With a LURCH,

With a wiggle,

With a Crunch

and a sway

9

His blanket he pulled
up tight over his head.

Was he safe in his bed-tent ...
or ... maybe instead ...

Should he let out a scream?
Should he let out a holler?

Or run down the hall ...
and warn his father?

That an *alien*,

monster,

space
creature,

zombie ....!

12

Might possibly be after his own ... dear ... MOMMY.

Oh, what should he do?
How should he go?

Should he
run
really fast?

Or sneak out
v-e-r-y
s-l-o-w-l-y ?

But every time he jumped out of
his bed and went running,

Those crafty monsters,
you know they're quite cunning,

They would vanish,
they would hide,
they would completely disappear,

By the time that his parents could
get very near.

His father would say something like,
"It's all in your head."
And his mother would say nothing,
but hug him instead,
And leave him alone again ...

In ... the ... dark,

in ... his ... bed.

Oh, next time he thought,
he'd do
something quite
different.

So he
pondered
And he planned
In his comfy warm bed-tent.

The very next night when the
creepies started crawling,
He stayed in his bed instead of
screaming or
bawling.

Slinking
under his covers
to the bottom of his bed,
He crept to the corner ...

and ...

POKED OUT HIS HEAD!

"Hi, Mister Monster!
How do you do?
My name is Terry,
Oh, am I frightening you?

Please, don't run away ...
I won't scream or cry,
Say ... are you an alien
from out of the sky?

Or just a monster who
lives under my bed?
Is your name Billy,
or Mary, or ... Fred?

23

Well, that creature took a step back,
with its five knees a-knocking,
Its purple eye glowing
and its green lips so shocking,

"My name is
   Oodle.
I come from
   a star.
It's really quite
   close.
It's not very far.

I live in the darkness,
I don't like the light.
That's why I always
come visiting at night.

But if you'll be my friend,
We could be quite chummy,
And I'd even fly you home with
me, some night, to visit my
mummy.

On the way
to my planet,
we can stop
off and visit ...

my friends, the Bamboozles,
who love to drink Fizzit.

You'll find when you drink it,
Fizzit's quite the sensation
Because it's flavor is
made with your imagination.

So think of a flavor, like
chocolate, cherry, or plum
And that's what your Fizzit
will surely become.

After guzzling our Fizzit
and finishing our play,
We'll thank those Bamboozles
and be on our way.

We'll fly in my spacecraft to
my planet Dimdoodle,

And be back here in
the morning after eating
Stardust Strudel."

The adventures were many
these two shared every night,
From Mars on the left
to Pluto on the right,

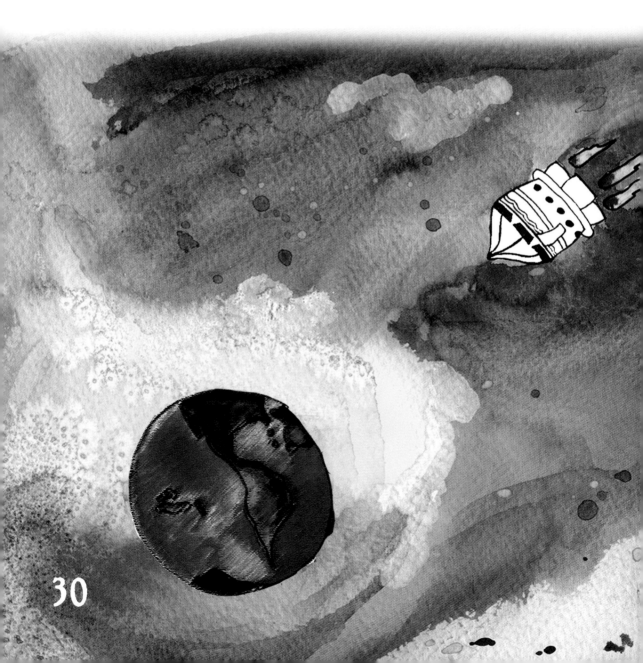

And Terry discovered
    after much, much ado,
That scary looking monsters
    can be best friends, too.

That five knees,
    and green lips,
    and a purple eye
    glowing
Can sometimes be
    someone who's
    really worth
    knowing.

31

But, you know, it's too bad
that parents sleep all through
the night ...

And *miss* meeting those monsters
who don't like the *light.* ⱺⱺ